THE STORY OF THE AVENGERS

Adapted by Thomas Macri
Illustrated by Mike Norton, Pat Olliffe, Val Semeiks, *and* Hi-Fi Design
Based on the Marvel comic book series The Mighty Avengers

New York

WWW.ABDOPUBLISHING.COM

Reinforced library bound edition published in 2015 by Spotlight, a division of ABDO PO Box 398166, Minneapolis, Minnesota 55439. Spotlight produces high-quality reinforced library bound editions for schools and libraries. Published by Marvel Press, an imprint of Disney Book Group.

Printed in the United States of America, North Mankato, Minnesota.
052014
072014

LIBRARY OF CONGRESS CATALOGING-IN-PUBLICATION DATA

This title was previously cataloged with the following information:

Macri, Thomas.
The story of the Avengers / adapted by Thomas Macri ; illustrated by Mike Norton... [et al.].
p. cm. -- (World of reading. Level 2)
Summary: Describes how a group of super heroes became the Avengers team.
1. Avengers (Fictitious characters)--Juvenile fiction. 2. Superheroes--Juvenile fiction. I. Mike Norton, ill. II. Title. III. Series.
PZ7.M24731Stc 2012
[E]--dc23

2012285589

978-1-61479-261-1 (Reinforced Library Bound Edition)

Spotlight

A Division of ABDO
www.abdopublishing.com

Super Villains did bad things.

But there was always a Super Hero somewhere to stop them.
Thor fought giants in Asgard.

On Earth, Hulk smashed.
He had great power.

Far away, Iron Man
used his blasts.

Around the world, Ant-Man
and Wasp rushed into action.

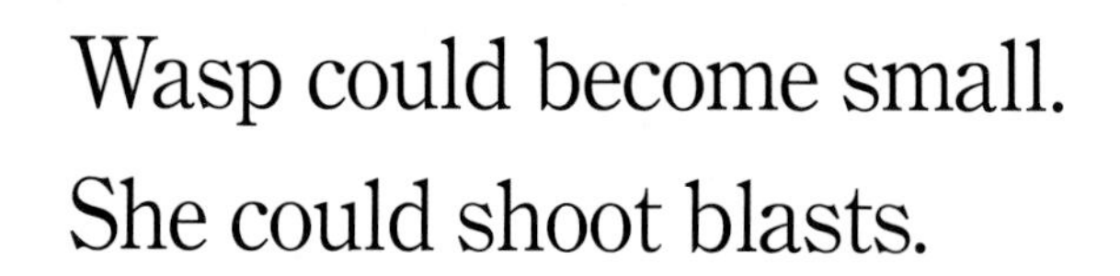

Wasp could become small.
She could shoot blasts.

Ant-Man could become small, too.
But he could also become big.
When he was big, he was Giant-Man!

One day a villain planned
something really bad.
The bad guy's name was Loki.

Loki's brother was Thor.
Thor was a Super Hero.
He had a great hammer.
It helped him beat bad guys.

Loki was jealous of Thor.
Loki used the Hulk to lure Thor.

Loki tricked people. He made them think the Hulk had smashed train tracks. He knew Thor would rush to the rescue.

Ant-Man and Wasp flew over.

So did Iron Man.

They met at the train.
Loki's brother, Thor, was there, too.

Iron Man, Ant-Man, and Wasp
flew off to find the Hulk.

But Thor went to find Loki.
He knew he was the real villain.

The heroes attacked the Hulk.

They thought he was a bad guy.

But Thor brought Loki to them.
He held him up.
He told them Loki was the real bad guy.

The Super Heroes fought Loki
and won!

They called it the Avengers!

They fought together.

They beat bad guys who were too tough to fight alone.

One battle took the team
to a frozen land.

There, the Avengers
spotted a man in ice.
Giant-Man swam to the man.
He grabbed him and brought
him back.

Iron Man used his rays to melt
the ice.
He had to be careful.
He didn't want to burn the man.

The man in the ice was
Captain America!

He was a hero from long ago.
He had a mighty shield.

Captain America was confused.
He had been lost for a long time.
He didn't know these Super Heroes.

Iron Man put a hand on his shoulder.

Suddenly, the Avengers were attacked.
The bad guys were all around them.

Cap's shield flew by.

He helped the Avengers beat
the bad guys!

The team was finally complete. Cap had joined them. Now, no one could ever beat them.

The world could always count on the Avengers!